SAWYER

Kathleen Ryder

About *Sawyer*

As heir to the largest toy company in the world, Sawyer Klauss is used to being in charge. What he is not used to, is children. When he is named guardian of two small boys, it is clear he is out of his depth. With limited options, Sawyer has no choice but to hire nanny Becca Parkes, even if she is the most annoying person he has ever met!

When Becca Parkes takes a job as a nanny for the month of December, she had no idea that she would be working for Sawyer Klauss, the most eligible bachelor in San Diego. Too bad he was also the most irritating person she had ever met!

With his busiest season fast approaching, can Becca and Sawyer work together to create a winning advertising campaign, give the boys the Christmas they deserve, and find a little Christmas magic for themselves, or will their differences lead to a December disaster?

DEDICATION

For my son, the very best thing about
Christmas are the memories I share
with you x

CHAPTER ONE
SAWYER

Sawyer looked around his penthouse apartment and sighed deeply, shaking his head slightly at the sight, a frown appearing on his face. He had no idea that children could be so catastrophically messy. He felt a sudden twinge of guilt as he remembered the mess that he and his brothers would often leave for his mother, or their nanny, to clean up for them, perhaps this was karma? He crossed to the small bar in the corner and poured himself a large scotch, sipping it as he looked out of the window, soaking in the San Diego skyline. He knew that he couldn't keep going like this, something would have to give. His family was counting on him, each December his campaign alone was responsible for bringing in millions of dollars in revenue for their company, and this year would be no different. While other lesser-known toy companies would launch their single Christmas campaign on the first day of November, the Klauss Brothers toy company, founded over three hundred years ago, would launch the first of their two campaigns, with the second launching the week before Christmas.

The Klauss Brothers Christmas campaign had become famous in itself and had a dedicated fanbase, eager for the next instalment. Unlike typical television and print commercials, the Klauss Brothers' Christmas campaign was a series of small movies and comics, all weaving together to form a larger movie or story each year. This was Sawyer's innovation, the first thing he had changed once he had taken over the advertising department of the business, and one which had proven highly successful. His clever advertising campaign had spurned merchandise of their own each year, the characters and scenes depicted on Christmas baubles and kitchenware just as popular as the actual commercials themselves. This year, Sawyer was having creativity issues. He had the first part of the campaign finished and already airing across television stations, but the second part, the ending, was still eluding him. Sawyer thought that recent events might be responsible for that.

Sawyer never expected to be named guardian of two little boys, but that is what happened. Eight weeks ago, Sawyer was in the middle of a board meeting with his family and other key staff members, when he had excused himself to take a call his receptionist had said was urgent. Two minutes later his entire world had shifted, and he had no idea which way was up anymore. His best friend Jonathan, the person he trusted most in the world after his own brothers, was dead. Jonathan and his wife Clarise had been driving into work when a drunk driver had run a red light and ploughed right into their car. Clarise had been killed instantly, and Jonathan had died at the scene. Sawyer had been named sole guardian of their two small boys, Samuel Jonathan and Maxwell

Sawyer, or Sam and Max as they were known, aged just two and three. It had been a tough transition, from fun uncle to responsible parent, and Sawyer had felt adrift ever since. His family had all offered to help him, but he had wanted to do this on his own, had wanted to honour Jonathan and their friendship by doing right by his children.

He downed his scotch and sank down onto the plush sofa, jumping up again suddenly. Why was it wet? He ripped the cushions off to see a half-spilled juice box hiding underneath, and despite the mess it had made, it made him smile.

Those two were utter rascals, and he knew that in years to come they would play all types of pranks on him. Sawyer was surprised to realise that he was looking forward to it. His love for the boys was never in doubt, he had been the first to visit when both had been born, having waited in the waiting room throughout both of their deliveries, just in case either Jonathan or Clarise had needed anything. That he would take the boys, love them, and raise them as a parent was never in doubt. He just didn't know how to, that was all. He had never been interested in babies as a small boy, despite being from a large family, he was far too interested in following his dad around to worry about babies. Now though, he wished that he had paid more attention to what it was that his mother and nanny had done, maybe then he wouldn't feel so very far out of his element.

He sighed again as he bent to pick up a random assortment of socks and toys, tossing them all into the washing basket for sorting later, or for disposal, depending on how grossed out Sawyer was with the prospect of cleaning them. He knew what he had to do, he had known it since Monday morning, when she had breezed in here without a care in the world, raising an eye at the mess strewn around, surreptitiously keeping her mouth closed as she had stepped over a bowl of cereal on the floor and made her way to the kitchen table to be interviewed. He needed a nanny, more specifically, he needed her, Becca Parkes. The fact that he was even admitting that to himself made his skin crawl. Becca Parkes was his mother's best friend's granddaughter, and she seemingly floated through life unburdened by responsibilities such as a job or a house. Sawyer had only met her once before, at a family Christmas party, and she had irked him no end with her carefree lifestyle. Sawyer just could not understand how someone wouldn't want to have a career, a home, or some direction in life.

Honestly, Becca Parkes was single-handedly the most annoying person that Sawyer had ever met! Unfortunately for him, she was also the only person available. It wasn't easy, trying to wrangle a nanny for a month's work over December, most of them already had jobs with holidaying families, or were spending the season at home with their own families. Becca had been his mother's suggestion, and as much as he had baulked at it, she was also the only one who had no prior commitments, the only one who could stay the entire month he required. In hindsight, the decision had already been made before he had interviewed her, he knew that. while Becca might live her life responsibility-free, she was good with kids, he knew that his mother would never suggest anyone who would bring harm to his children. Giving up on his attempt at tidying up the house, Sawyer crossed to his home office and switched on his laptop, sending Becca a quick email advising her that she had the job, and that he needed her to be here by Sunday afternoon at the latest. With that out of the way, he went and checked on Sam and Max, both sleeping soundly in the guest room, before turning in for the night himself.

CHAPTER TWO
BECCA

As soon as the penthouse door swung open, Becca knew why her grandmother had been so vague when it had come to the particulars of the position vacant. Had she known that the job was for Sawyer Klauss, she would never have agreed to go to the interview. Still, if there was any consolation, it seemed as if he was just as irritated to have her there as she was being there. Good, she smiled to herself, let him squirm, he deserved it after the appalling way in which he had treated her at last year's family Christmas party. She usually didn't attend the party, in fact, she considered it a Christmas gift to herself to stay away, but last year she had succumbed to her grandmother's pleas, and had attended with her. Becca had never understood how her grandmother and Sawyer's mum had become such firm friends, but they had, despite being polar opposites. While Sawyer's mum had raised a large family of nine or ten boys, Becca honestly couldn't count how many Klauss brothers there were running around, her grandmother had raised a single daughter, Becca's mum.

When Sawyer's mother had finished raising her family, she had joined her husband in building up their business, helping to make it what it is today. In contrast, Becca's mother had been barely sixteen when Becca had been born and had left her with her grandmother one night and never came back. Her grandmother had put any ambitions she might have had to one side and raised Becca as best she could. Becca owed her grandmother everything, so if she had to sit through one family Christmas with the richest people she knew, or if she had to take a job working for one of them, then so be it. Becca would do almost anything for her grandmother, even if it meant curtailing her carefree lifestyle for a few weeks in order to spend December working. At least she would be spending all of her free time with her grandmother, something Becca always missed while she was away travelling the world.

The job interview had gone about as well as Becca could have expected it to, and she swung past the bakery on the way back to her grandmother's apartment, picking up her favourite treat for afternoon tea. Her grandmother loved meringues and this way,

when Becca told her that she didn't expect to get the job, it would sweeten the blow so to speak. She didn't know that Sawyer had children, he obviously had no wife in his life if he was seeking a nanny, but Becca couldn't understand why anyone with kids would need to hire a nanny to take care of them over Christmas, after all, Christmas is nothing if not a time for family, a sentiment that she shared with her grandmother as they enjoyed their meringues out on her balcony.

"Becca, really, you don't know, he didn't tell you?" Her grandmother sounds surprised.

"We spoke about the requirements of the job, gran, that was all. Keep the children out of his office, out of his way, and keep them quiet."

"He said that?" Her grandmother sounded shocked.

"No," Becca admitted, "my words, not his."

"Becca," her grandmother warned, "Sawyer would do anything for those children, he isn't your mother."

"I know that," Becca grumbled, not quite believing her grandmother.

"I mean it, young lady. Don't go making trouble where there is none."

"All right, gran, I just think it is wrong, hiring a nanny to watch your children for Christmas so that you can what, work some more? What will that teach them? That work always comes first? Another generation of corporate workaholics with no time to appreciate life."

"How Sawyer chooses to raise those kids is none of your business Becca, but trust me, he is still learning, they are all still finding their place."

"They are two and three, how long does it take to learn how to parent?"

"Sawyer isn't their father, Becca, at least, he wasn't until a couple of months ago. His best friend and his wife died in a car crash, leaving Sawyer as the sole guardian of those little boys. He adores them as if they were his own, but it has been hard for him, losing his friend, and transitioning from fun uncle to responsible dad."

"Gran!" Becca was horrified. "You should have told me."

"Why? You didn't say anything did you, Becca?"

"No, gran, I didn't say anything, but the house was a mess, I thought...I judged him. If I had known what had happened, I would have been kinder in my thoughts." Becca was interrupted by the sound of her phone beeping, alerting her to an email. A quick glance at the screen showed that it was from Sawyer, and she opened it, skimming through the text. "Huh. I got the job." To say she was surprised would be an understatement, Becca was stunned! She really thought that Sawyer did not like her, he must be quite desperate after all.

"Well, there you go, that's wonderful!" Her grandmother clapped her hands together, a large smile forming on her mouth. "Now you can help them."

"Hmm. I'm not a miracle worker gran."

"We'll see, I know you'll be good for that family, trust me on this."

CHAPTER THREE
SAWYER

Pushing his chair away from his desk with a sigh, Sawyer rubbed his temples. The decision to work from his office at home for a few days had seemed like a good idea, especially while Becca settled in and the children became accustomed to her, but he was starting to realise that the idea was flawed. Despite being in his office for over an hour now, he had yet to manage to formulate any ideas, his cursor blinking up at him from the blank page, taunting him with every blink. As another loud shrill pierced the air, he rose with a sigh, crossing to his office door and yanking it open, expecting to see a bloodbath, instead, stopping dead in his tracks at the sight of Sam and Max jumping head first off the plush leather sofa and onto a pile of pillows on the floor.

"What on earth is going on out here?" Sawyer asked, hands on hips.

"Uncle Sawyer, we play diving," Max informed him in a sombre voice. Sawyer's heart constricted at the sound, he wished Max was more lively, more carefree, not so weighed down by his grief and loss.

"Diving, huh," Sawyer caught Sam mid-flight, "that sounds like fun. Maybe we could all go down to the pool and dive in the water?" As much as he was loathed to take time off work, he wasn't very creative today, his mojo had stalled on him, or maybe deserted him altogether, only time would tell, and he would much rather the boys learned to dive in the water, where it was relatively safe, as opposed to his penthouse floor, which would do nothing to cushion a fall.

"The pool?" Becca's voice was hesitant. "Won't that be too cold?"

"It's heated," he rolled his eyes at her, "give me some credit, as if I would take the boys if it was cold, and risk them getting sick. Honestly," he shook his head, "believe it or not, I do know what I am doing. Now," he turned back to the boys, who were watching him with wide eyes, "who's coming swimming?" The question, while rhetorical, was met with a chorus of shouts and happy squeals. "Come on, let's go get changed into our swimmers."

"Um, Sawyer," Becca's voice stopped him halfway out of the room, "I don't have a swimming costume."

"Can you swim?" Sawyer turned to look at Becca, his gaze raking up and down her body unashamedly. He hadn't thought to ask her when he had interviewed her, after all, she would only be here for a month, and most of her skills would be irrelevant.

"Yes, I just didn't bring my swimmers with me, being winter, I didn't think they would be needed."

"Okay, go through to the third spare room, well, the only one that is really spare now that you and the boys are here, and look in the closet for a swimsuit."

"Seriously?"

"I keep a range of swimsuits here."

"I see." Her answer had Sawyer barking with laughter.

"Despite what you may think Becca, I keep a range of swimsuits in all sizes, for men, women, and children here, I entertain a lot, and my family is large, there is always someone who has forgotten their suit." Not bothering to wait for her to pick her jaw up off the floor, Sawyer turned and continued to lead the boys from the room.

It didn't take Sawyer long to get Sam and Max dressed in swimmers and gather up towels and floaties, the three of them waiting near the penthouse lift for Becca to join them. The moment Sawyer saw her he regretted inviting her along. Dressed in a retro-inspired dusty pink, backless, halter top one-piece swimsuit, with a plunging V-neck, Becca looked like Christmas morning all wrapped up. Good grief! What was wrong with him? He gave himself a mental shake. This was Becca he was looking at, Becca who had no life direction, Becca who didn't even come home for Christmas, Becca who annoyed him, Becca who hated him, Becca who currently worked for him. This was not a woman with a life plan or goals or anything in common with him, this was not someone who he should get involved with, even if he had the time, which he absolutely did not. Internal pep talk over, he ushered the small group into the lift, letting Max push the button for the pool, refusing to meet Becca's eye, not trusting himself to remain silent. The ride down to the pool level was punctuated by the excited chatter of Sam and Max, who, prior to becoming orphans, would spend most weekends here with their parents and Sawyer, not having had a swimming pool in their own apartment complex.

The swimming pool complex took up an entire level in the apartment building and was more like a swimming grotto than a traditional swimming pool. Resembling a large, man-made lagoon, the grotto was made up of large rock waterfalls, with hidden nooks and caverns that were large enough to swim into. There were seating areas, mood lighting, a therapy spa, large caves hiding secret lounging areas, a bar, water features, areas to eat, smaller man-made tropical islands with hammocks, and even a splash pool for those with little children. The entire set-up was heated salt water, surrounded by a white sandy beach and patrolled by around-the-clock lifeguards. Sawyer led the boys towards a cluster of sun lounges on the beach and set down their towels and floaties. Sam happily let himself be led over to the splash pad by Becca, while Sawyer took Max into the pool. Max had always been apprehensive around the water, but with Sawyer holding him tightly to his chest, Max was content to simply be held in the water, stretching his arms out and running his fingers through the water.

They stayed at the pool for the rest of the day, ordering faux tropical cocktails in a variety of vivid colours, the boys slurping on their icy treats with gusto, and snacking on French fries and ribbon sandwiches. They only left when Sam started to doze off on Becca's shoulder, Sawyer carrying a tired Max, promising the youngster that they would come back another day, his heart constricting when Max snuggled closer still, little hands clenching at Sawyer's shirt.

"I love you, Uncle Sawyer."

"I love you too, Max, so much."

CHAPTER FOUR
BECCA

"Sawyer?" Becca knocked tentatively on the office doorjamb, peering her head through the open door.

"Hmm," Sawyer looked up from his paperwork, a small frown on his forehead.

"Do you have a moment, it isn't urgent," she hastened to add before he started to worry, "I just wanted to talk to you about Sam and Max when you have some time." Becca smiled across the room, hoping it projected a look of assurance.

"Now's fine, I wasn't making much headway with this campaign anyway." Sawyer tossed down his pencil and leant forwards towards Becca.

"Writer's block, or whatever the design equivalent is?" Becca sat on the chair opposite Sawyer.

"Something like that, I just can't seem to get the design to flow," Sawyer shrugged.

"I'm sorry, I don't know anything about the mechanics of product or advertising design, but maybe a change of scenery would help?" She suggested sweetly.

"Oh yeah," Sawyer grinned, "what did you have in mind?"

"A trip to the mall," Becca grinned back.

"The mall?!" Becca actually laughed out loud at the expression on Sawyer's face. "Don't look so horrified, Sawyer, you'll be okay, we'll stick together, I promise."

"Okay, I'll bite, what's at the mall?"

"Shops," Becca answered matter of fact. "I know that this is your penthouse and that I am only here a short while, so please, tell me to butt out if you think I am overstepping, but..." Becca trailed off.

"But..." Sawyer prompted.

"Why are the boys still sleeping in the spare room?" She blurted out in a rush. "Why don't they have their own room?"

"What do you mean? They are in their own room."

"I mean, the room is so sterile, it still looks like the spare room, with twin beds simply shoved in. There are no signs that Sam and Max live there, no toys, no colourful rugs, no trinkets, no murals on the walls, it is just so barren.

"I see, you think I should redecorate?"

"I know a children's room doesn't really fit into the aesthetic of a penthouse apartment, but those boys have been through a lot, too much for someone so young, I think that living in such a sterile, cold, environment, isn't doing them any good, not in the long run. They need vibrancy and familiarity, they need their things, their own space, they need to feel that they belong here, permanently, not just temporarily." Becca defended, hoping that she wouldn't be fired on the spot.

"I know. You're right, I know you are, the truth is," he ran his hand through his hair, "I haven't been able to go back to their house, not yet, I just can't. My housekeeper goes there once a week to dust, but otherwise, everything is just as they left it that morning."

"Oh, Sawyer," Becca's heart ached at his admission, "I'm so very sorry, I can't even imagine the pain you must be in, I imagine just seeing the boys is hard at times."

"Unimaginably so," Sawyer cleared his throat, "but Sam and Max will never know, as far as they are concerned, they are my whole world now, nothing I will ever do will be as important as raising them."

Sawyer rose and walked around his desk, Becca rising to stand next to him.

"So, if brightening up their room will help them know they are here to stay, then let's do it."

"Yeah?" Becca tried and failed, to keep the excitement out of her voice.

"Shopaholic much?" Sawyer chuckled.

"Full disclosure, Sawyer? I never had this growing up."

"What?"

"My own space, connections. My mother dumped me shortly after I was born, I've never seen her since, although I know my grandmother hears from her every now and then. She married and had more kids, but never reached out to me. I learnt to be resilient from my grandmother, but I know it came at a price, I keep people, adults, at a distance, I don't want to get hurt. I guess I just want to help Sam and Max keep their connections, to have that security. I know you think I'm carefree, I'm not really, I travel to collect memories, but also to avoid having to take bigger risks, to actually connect with people, to form relationships, to risk hurt. Inside, I guess I'll always be that kid who wasn't wanted."

"I misjudged you, Becca, I'm sorry," Sawyer apologised.

"Don't," Becca shook her head, "I think we both misjudged each other. Maybe we can start again? Truce?" She held her hand out to Sawyer.

"I'd like that," Sawyer took her hand in his, shaking. "Now, let's wrangle those boys and head to the mall." Becca expected Sawyer's enthusiasm to wane, or to be short-lived but was pleasantly surprised to see him actually enjoying himself. She wondered if he had ever really spent time just wandering around, shopping, or if he had someone else do it for him. They hired a cute car-shaped trolley for the boys to ride in, complete with mini steering wheels, the boys pretending to drive their way around the shopping mall. Although it was fun, and Becca could almost imagine herself doing this regularly, they didn't linger, the boys growing tired. They enjoyed a nice lunch together before heading home, the boys both falling asleep in the car on the drive home. Sawyer carried them up to bed while Becca unloaded the car, the heavier items would be delivered later that day.

While the boys napped, Becca unpacked and sorted all of their purchases, and with the store delivering the rest of the purchases as the boys were waking up, she was ready to get started on the room makeover. The boys thought it was great fun, helping her to decorate and arrange items, Sawyer doing the heavy lifting, swapping out the generic beds for two fire engine shaped beds, and the generic wardrobe for one that looked as if it were made from fire truck ladders. Colourful shelves, new linen, a small bookcase, and enough toys to open a toy store all helped to complete the look, the boys dashing from item to item, oohing and aahing over every small detail. It had been a great day, Becca reflected, loving the way the boys were exploring their new surroundings, and she was glad that she had suggested this. If only there was some way that she could help Sawyer as well, now that would be the best Christmas gift that she could give him.

Despite her resolve to not get involved, Becca suddenly realised that she wanted to do this for him, she wanted to help Sawyer through this Christmas. Surely, she could do that, as his friend, and still stay emotionally aloof, emotionally protected. How hard could it be?

CHAPTER FIVE
SAWYER

Yesterday had been more enjoyable than Sawyer had thought that it would be, he knew that had a lot to do with the company. Try as he may, he couldn't fail but notice Becca's every move. It was crazy, he had known her for years, but had never actually taken the time to get to know her. Maybe if he had, they would have dated, maybe he would have kissed her goodnight. Instead, he had been blind, and now that he was able to see her clearly, it was too late, she was his employee, for however short a time, and while he might be a lot of things, improper was not one of them. Maybe it was just as well, he had Sam and Max to think about now, they were his whole world, he wouldn't be able to give a relationship the time it deserved. In any case, he had never been a fan of casual dating. No, if he was to embark on a relationship now, he wanted to know that it would be for keeps, forever, as corny as that sounded. He wanted someone who would be there, not just for him, but for Sam and Max as well, always, and as a mother, not as a stepmother or someone only half aware of them. If that meant he was doomed to stay single, then so be it. He had enough trouble as it was, finding time to do things, maybe staying single was his destiny?

Sawyer was restless, he knew he should be trying to get this campaign finished, or even started, but he just couldn't focus. The deadline loomed over him, due in only three days, he knew he had to knuckle down, their entire Christmas launch hinged on his two-part campaign, if there was no part two, there would be endless upset and disappointed customers, and that was simply not a scenario he was prepared to entertain. Maybe he should have taken his mother's advice? Skipped this year, just run with a normal, single commercial campaign, but he had been certain that he could cope, it was the very reason he had hired Becca, to help with Max and Sam so that he could finish the campaign. Instead, she was as much of a distraction as the boys. Maybe he needed a change of scenery? It certainly couldn't hurt, could it?

"Max, Sam?" Sawyer followed the sound of laughter until he found the boys, smiling at the sight that met him, Sam and Max looking through Christmas books with Becca. "I thought we might go and see Santa today, would you like that?"

"Sawyer, that's a great idea, but will we get in? The stores all have huge lines this year." Becca rose and helped Sam and Max to put the books away.

"We'll go to Klauss's Toy Emporium," Sawyer shrugged, "we have the best Santa grotto anyway, and we'll get priority treatment, no queues for the boss," he shot Becca a wink.

"Sawyer! You can't do that, those kids have been waiting in line forever."

"Don't worry, Becca, no one will miss their turn. I'll let you in on a secret.

When Santa stops for lunch the grotto and waiting line is closed off by rich velvet curtains. Then Santa number two comes on and sees employees and their families only. One of the perks of working for us. Our employees don't miss out on family traditions, and none of the public feels cheated, it's a win-win."

"Huh, that's actually really very thoughtful. In that case, let's go!" Becca's blunt assessment of his business character brought his laugh to the surface, it was refreshing, as was her sense of what was right towards others, especially during the festive season, the busiest, and generally speaking, the most impatient time of the year.

As Sawyer walked Becca and the boys into the back entrance of Klauss's Toy Emporium, he was filled with a sense of pride. This would be their legacy when they were older, just as it was his. He started working for his father when he was fourteen, as did all of his brothers, working themselves up from the bottom, despite what some people thought. It was how they learnt the ropes, how they knew what each section was responsible for. This had been Sawyer's first store he had worked in, and it remained his favourite. He had stocked shelves, tended the cash register, served customers, ordered stock, swept floors, and even cleaned when it had been needed. He had learnt all of the roles and had earned the respect of those he had worked with. he couldn't wait until Sam and Max were old enough to share this with. He led the trio through a series of secret corridors, past offices and rooms filled with rows upon rows of toys yet to be released, smiling as Max's eyes grew rounder and rounder until Sawyer thought he might pass out from excitement.

"Sawyer!" A voice called out behind him, the group turning at the shout.

"Dad," Sawyer embraced the older man warmly. "I didn't know you'd be in today."

"Your mum sent me to collect the toys to take to the toy drive, I'm under strict instructions to bring them all home so that she can wrap them before delivering them. Sam, Max," he held his arms out to his two newest grandsons, hugging them as if they had always been his. "What are my favourite grandsons doing here?"

"Dad, they are your only grandsons," Sawyer reminded him with an eye roll.

"Semantics," his father brushed him off with a sly grin, "now, how would you like to help grandpa choose some presents for charity?"

"I'm sorry grandpa," Max sounded so regretful it was almost comical, "Sam and I are going to see Santa."

"Santa!" His father boomed. "Well, come on then, let's go," he scooped Sam up onto his hip and took Max's hand in his free hand, "I know Santa well, he gets all of his toys from us you know." Sawyer and Becca shared a smile as his father led them down to Santa's grotto, regaling the boys with stories of Santa and the many adventures he had had with him.

This is what Christmas was all about, Sawyer realised, sharing traditions, telling stories, and generations connected through acts of togetherness and memory-making. Their visit to Santa was a huge success. The secret Santa session, as the staff referred to them, was already in full swing, and despite being happy to wait, Sawyer found themselves pushed to the front of the queue.

"Oh no, please," Sawyer protested, "we can wait, honestly, you have all been waiting a lot longer than us."

"Sawyer," the floor manager spoke up, "I know I speak for all of us here today, please, let us do this for you, a small gesture from us to you, for Christmas, for Max and Sam, we know how much you have all been through, let us do this small thing for you today."

"Thank you," Sawyer shook the man's hand, overwhelmed by his speech. He forgot sometimes that he meant as much to his employees as they meant to him. Sam and Max had a wonderful visit with Santa, who happily corroborated their grandfather's tales, and after hearing their wishes and having their photos taken, gave the boys a brightly wrapped gift each, much to their delight.

"What?" Sawyer shrugged at Becca's raised eyebrows at Sam and Max's gifts, a train set and a metre-long fire engine with lights and sounds. "This is a toy store, and our employees work hard, it is our pleasure to treat their children at Christmas time."

"You, Sawyer Klauss, are a real-life Father Christmas," Becca whispered softly, elbowing him in the side with a smile. They were making their way back to his father's office, Max chatting away to his grandpa about his fire engine and his new bedroom, his eyes sparkling. He should have done this days ago, he should have been here every day, this is where his inspiration was, with the people he worked with, those he had shared history with, where his story had started. Sawyer stopped dead in his tracks, his father and Becca stopping to look at him questioningly.

"I need to get home," he spoke quickly, excitedly, "I know what the second half of the campaign looks like now, I have it!"

"Go," his father spoke first, "I'll run Becca Sam and Max home when the boys have had enough."

"Thank you, Dad."

"Sawyer, it's good to have you back," his father smiled at him.

"It's good to be back, Dad, thank you."

Sawyer played Christmas carols on the way home, the festive feeling from the store having seeped through to his very core. He loved Christmas; this really was his favourite time of the year. After he finished getting this campaign done, he was going to treat Becca, Sam, and Max to a day out, somewhere nice, a theme park perhaps, to take in the Christmas parades. Yes, that's what he'll do. He thought over his plans for the rest of the drive home, happy to be able to share this with them. He grabbed a bottle of water from the fridge before going to his office, he knew from experience that when he started a project he wouldn't surface until it was finished, not even for meals. He fired up his computer, thrilled with finally being able to start. It wasn't long until he was in the groove, soft carols playing in the background to set the scene, his electric fireplace on for ambience. He worked in silence, unaware of how much time had passed until he turned to stretch and caught sight of the clock on the fireplace mantel. It was well after midnight, Becca had obviously brought the boys home and the three of them had been quiet, which had allowed him to work uninterrupted this whole time. A feeling of gratefulness surged through Sawyer, and he turned back to his project, eager to continue.

There, it was finished, and the campaign had been emailed over to his team for distribution across all channels in time for the first news cycle. Usually, Sawyer would show his family, or his father at least, so that they had an idea of what to expect, but this year he had opted not to. This was going to be his gift to them, a thank you of sorts. Sawyer thought this was his best campaign yet, he couldn't wait to see everyone's reactions. The campaign started in a toy store, two young boys out with their grandfather, surrounded by aisles of wonderous toys stretching as far as the eye could see. They see the boys carefully choosing toys and having them wrapped nicely before they place them into the store's charity donation box, all the while listening as their grandfather regales them with stories of Christmas when he was younger. As the trio start to leave, they spot a figure at the end of the aisle, stepping out of the shadow to reveal Santa, a trolley full of toys. The young boys watch in awe as Santa embraces their grandfather, exclaiming how happy he is to see him again. The commercial ends with a fade-out to Sawyer, seated in his armchair in front of the fire, speaking directly to the camera, one on one.

He started by wishing all of their loyal customers a Merry Christmas and then he did something he had never done before. He addressed them as he would a close friend, sharing the loss of his best friend, and introducing the two newest members of his family via photographs. He asked them to respect the privacy of his newly formed family, to keep the boys in their thoughts this Christmas, and to hold their own children a little closer this year. Sawyer went on to say that this is what Christmas was all about, family, generations connected. It was the perfect end to the campaign.

CHAPTER SIX
BECCA

"I'm hosting a Christmas party of sorts tonight, on the upper level and the roof terrace, remember I told you about it the other day?" Sawyer poured himself a coffee as he spoke, his back to Becca, unaware of her eyes roving across his back and down over his firm legs.

"I remember," Becca confirmed, averting her eyes back to Sam as Sawyer turned around, pretending that she was utterly engrossed in watching Sam as he attempted to manoeuvre a forkful of chicken salad to his mouth. "Don't worry, Sawyer, everything will be fine. The boys and I have our evening all planned out," she sent him her most dazzling smile, "we're going to have a picnic and watch a movie together in the den, then after they are in bed, I have a date with my new book. They aren't going to be in anyone's way, I promise."

"That's not what I was worried about" he sighed. "They aren't some novelty to be trotted out and fawned over."

"I know. I've got this, trust me, they'll be fine."

"You'll come to find me if they need me?" Although he phrased it as a question, Becca knew it was anything but.

"I promise." With a nod at the trio at the table, he wandered off, no doubt to sort out last-minute arrangements for his party tonight. Becca thought it was endearing how much he wanted to shield the boys from the inevitable publicity and notoriety that came with being in his sphere, but she wondered if he knew that eventually, they would need to learn how to deal with the press and events, instead of simply avoiding them. She wondered if he had ever wanted to simply run away, to not show up to an event, to just be incognito sometimes. Maybe she would ask him, now that they were over their initial awkwardness and almost...What? What were they? Could she call them friends? In a way, maybe. After all, they had known each other for most of their lives, through their parents and grandparents, and often attended family gatherings at the same time. Maybe after this, she could actually be friends with him, that might be nice, and they would always have Sam and Max in common. Yes, she decided, they were friends.

They were friends, she reminded herself a few hours later when Sawyer had walked out to the kitchen dressed in his suit pants and crisp white shirt, tie hanging around his neck, his hair still damp from the shower. Without thinking Becca had stepped closer and taken his tie in her hands, deftly tying it in a classic Windsor knot, smoothing out his lapels with her palms. She had the overwhelming urge to reach up and kiss him, the realisation shocking her and causing her to jump backwards.

"There, all done." Was it just her or did her voice sound husky?

"Thank you." Sawyer looked at her curiously but thankfully made no further comment. What was wrong with her? For goodness' sake, it hadn't been that long ago that she hated Sawyer, now she was thinking about kissing him?! It hadn't been that long since her last date, had it? Truthfully, Becca couldn't actually remember when it had been, maybe between Valentine's Day and Easter? In any case, it had been nondescript and hadn't resulted in a second date. And, she conceded, she hadn't actually hated Sawyer, rather, she had hated everything that she thought he had represented, had stood for, although she had now come to realise that she had been completely wrong about him in every way.

Still, whether she was wrong about him or not was irrelevant, she was his employee and she would not harbour any feelings other than friendship towards him, even if he did look edible in his tailored suit. With a mammoth effort, Becca pushed all thoughts of Sawyer to the back of her mind and focused on setting up the den for her evening with the boys. They were getting an early start, the boys having a very firm bedtime, and Becca knew that they would most likely already be in bed sound asleep by the time Sawyer's party was in full swing, his guests not due to arrive before eight that evening. Becca enjoyed a lovely evening of snuggles with the boys, both of who fell asleep at her sides, traces of their ice cream dessert still evident on the corners of their lips. She carried them carefully through to their room and changed them for bed, slipping them into their toddler beds and tucking them in carefully, dropping a soft kiss onto their heads before closing the door quietly behind her.

Becca was in the kitchen, singing softly to herself when she suddenly felt as if she was being watched. Looking up from the open fridge, her warm brown eyes met icy blue pools, the face housing them staring at her with disdain.

"Can I help you?"

"Unlikely," the face snorted. "I'm Sonja, Sawyer's fiancé."

"Oh, nice to meet you," Becca smiled across at the woman, hoping it didn't appear as fake as it felt, "the boys have just gone to bed for the night, but you can still sneak in and see them if you'd like to."

"Good heavens no, why on earth would I want to do that?" Sonja laughed, the sound petty and mocking.

"You're marrying Sawyer, their legal guardian. You will be their mother for all intents and purposes, I would have thought that you would have wanted to develop and nurture that relationship as often as possible." Something about Sonja rubbed Becca the wrong way, she hoped it wasn't just because she had said that she was Sawyer's fiancé, after all, why should Becca care if he was engaged or not?

"I wouldn't expect you to understand," Sonja spoke scathingly, "but when I marry Sawyer, those children won't be a factor in our lives, believe me."

"Really? Is that so?" Sawyer drawled from the doorway, causing Becca to jump and Sonja to flush a deep red.

"Ah...I'll just, um, go elsewhere," Becca stuttered, edging towards the kitchen doorway and scooting around Sawyer.

"Wait right there," Sawyer commanded just as Becca was about to dash out of the door and disappear to her room and her book, away from the awkwardness of the kitchen. "There is no reason for you to dash away just because one of my guests is being rude." Becca's mouth gaped open at his comment, and she dared sneak a peek at Sonja, her face looking thunderous.

"I'm hardly a guest, Sawyer."

"No, you're right, you're a work colleague, not a guest, and despite what you may like to believe in your fantasies, Sonja, I am not now nor will I ever be, interested in pursuing a relationship with you of any kind outside of a professional one."

Becca didn't know where to look, she wished the floor would open up and swallow her whole, and she wasn't even involved in the conversation, she was merely a spectator.

"Sawyer, I'm-"

"The next words had better be an apology for lying, Sonja. Our fathers may be old friends, but don't think for one second that that will save you from being fired."

"Fine," Sonja huffed, folding her arms over her chest, "you can't blame me for trying, Sawyer, you know our fathers had hoped for a merger."

"I'm sorry that you feel the constant need to prove yourself to your father, Sonja, I truly am, and I don't say this to hurt you, but you must know that I don't see you in that way, I never have. You are a wonderful woman, Sonja, and one day you will meet a man who will love you for you, someone you won't need to change for, I promise you," Sawyer kissed her on the cheek. "Now, shall we get back to the party?"

"I'm sorry," Sonja addressed Becca as Sawyer led her back upstairs, "enjoy the rest of your night."

CHAPTER SEVEN
SAWYER

It had been three days since the second half of his Christmas campaign had launched, and according to his father, it was a roaring success. Sales figures for the week showed a six hundred per cent increase from the same time the previous year, but more importantly, their stores had seen an increase in the number of shoppers coming in together with older family members, sharing memories and hunting for Santa. There had also been a flurry of people leaving condolences and Christmas messages for Sam and Max both in-store and across social media, not that Sawyer had seen them. With his campaign finalised and released, he was officially enjoying the Christmas holidays with Becca and the boys. Today was the day he had decided to surprise them with a trip to a local theme park. When Sam and Max came out to the kitchen for breakfast, Sawyer already had the table set up with balloons and licensed merchandise, excitedly telling them where they were going for the day. Sawyer wasn't sure who was more excited, Becca or the boys, it was cute when they were all giddy and happy.

It didn't take long to drive the short distance to the theme park, the boys having dressed in record time in cute matching costumes that Sawyer had bought them, especially for the occasion. He had wanted to buy one for Becca as well but had chickened out, not quite sure he was ready to see her dressed up as a princess. As they wandered the park, Sawyer caught sight of them all in a store window, the reflection making his breath catch. They looked like a family, a real family, happy and laughing together. It was a funny feeling, a longing of sorts, whenever he looked at

Becca. Not the kind of longing that was easily sated by some snatched kisses, but rather a longing for the mundane, for the everyday, with her. It was a startling revelation. He wondered if it was merely a proximity issue, would he feel differently once she returned home? Watching her laugh with Max as they chose a helium balloon to buy, he had to admit what he had already known. Somehow, she had weaselled her way past his defences and into his heart. Or maybe he had let his defences down for her? He wasn't sure anymore. One thing he did know, was that he was running out of time, she would be returning home soon and there would be no more family outings or memories made with the boys, not together in any case. Sawyer would take what he could, he would make today so perfect it was never forgotten.

They spent the day snacking on food on a stick, enjoying the rides together, and buying trinkets the boys had taken a fancy to. They met characters, saw a fun show, and were even immortalised in caricature form. It had been a perfect day Sawyer thought, as they finally headed towards the park exit, Sam already fast asleep in his stroller, Max snuggled against his chest, utterly worn out from their day's adventures.

"Hey, Sawyer, who's the chick?" The flash of a camera had Sawyer scowling.

"Ignore them," he bit out to Becca, whose eyes were wide.

"Hey, Sam, Max, how about a picture?" Sawyer held Max's head firmly against his chest and away from the prying eyes of the paparazzi, relieved that Sam was sleeping in his stroller, covered with a sunshade. Park security had joined forces now to surround Sawyer and Becca and the boys, ushering them through the crowd towards the safety of the main building. "Max? Come on, Max, one smile, one picture?" The reporter would not give up. "Hey, lady, what's it like, working for Sawyer? Are you dating? Lovers? Is he generous? Come on, help a guy out, it's Christmas. Name your price, anything you want, it's yours if you call me." He shoved a card towards Becca, who took it with a frown.

CHAPTER EIGHT
BECCA

"Does that happen a lot to you?" She couldn't help but ask. It had been a perfect day, and she hated to ruin it now, but she was genuinely curious if the press was the reason that he was still single, or if it was a personal choice. Why she was so keen to know, she didn't want to admit to herself just yet.

"Sometimes," Sawyer nodded, started up the car and pulling out of the carpark. "It must be hard on you."

"I'm used to it," he shrugged.

"Is that why you're single?" Becca blurted out, blushing slightly at her lack of tact. Sawyer surprised her by laughing.

"You never cease to surprise me, but no, that is not why I am single. I just haven't met the right person yet, as cliched as that sounds."

"Oh," Becca wasn't quite sure what to make of that. "So, you have a type then?" Seriously, she needed to learn to keep her mouth shut, she had no idea what had happened to her inhibitions this afternoon.

"Of course, don't you?" He shot her a sideways glance.

"Sure," Becca thought quickly, "suburban history teachers, dependable, reliable."

"You're a terrible liar," Sawyer laughed.

"Fine," Becca admitted, "I prefer broody millionaires who value family more than work, who feel deeply, who take in children and love them and nurture them as their own," she finished quietly, wondering if she would be fired in the morning.

"I prefer spunky, outspoken women who tell me how it is, without fear. Women who step in to help care for children over Christmas, women who have been deeply hurt but yet still give others so much without expectation," Sawyer spoke slowly. Becca couldn't move, she wasn't even sure how she was still breathing, her heart felt as if it was about to jump out of her chest. Sawyer liked her, she was the one that he crushed over. She snuck a peek in his direction, a smile on her face when he turned and looked at her, sending her a wink that had her toes curling. They drove the rest of the way in silence, each lost in their own thoughts. Once home, they carried the boys inside, still sound asleep, and put them into bed for the night.

Shutting the boy's bedroom door behind her, Becca found herself face to face with Sawyer, and was suddenly nervous, her tongue darting out to lick her lips, as his eyes followed its path.

"Becca," Sawyer stepped closer and cupped her face gently in both of his hands, bringing his mouth down to hers, his tongue softly parting her lips, entering her mouth with exquisite slowness, drawing a deep sigh from her lips before breaking the kiss. "I want this," Sawyer punctuated each word with a soft kiss across her jawline and down her neck, "I want you."

"Sawyer, I'm...I mean, I've never..." Becca felt the heat of humiliation stain her cheeks, not quite sure how to tell Sawyer what she wanted to.

"Becca, are you a virgin?" Sawyer stilled against her.

"Yes," she whispered, squeezing her eyes shut against the rejection she knew would follow. Instead of stepping away from her, Sawyer tilted her face upwards and looking into her eyes, lowered his mouth to claim hers once again in a kiss that left her insides reeling.

"Will you stay with me, Becca?"

"Yes, I want to stay, I want you," she answered honestly. With a soft growl, he scooped her up into his arms and headed down the hallway to his bedroom.

When Becca woke the following morning, the bed was empty, a note left on Sawyer's pillow telling her that he had taken the boys to the park for a little while, that they wouldn't be gone long, that he missed her already. She took the time to shower and dress, stepping out onto the balcony to answer her ringing phone, hoping it was Sawyer telling her they were nearly home.

"No, I can't talk right now, I'm sorry, I'm with Sawyer. How much? Are you serious? Wow, okay, that's a lot of money. Yes, yes, I'll meet you, where? The café? Sure, sounds great, just give me half an hour or so, I need to get the boys ready first. Okay, bye." Becca hung up the phone and turned around, shrieking in surprise when she saw Sawyer lounging against the doorjamb, arms crossed over his chest, watching her through hooded eyes. "You almost gave me a heart attack," she accused with a smile, walking closer to reach up and kiss his lips in a good morning, frowning when he didn't respond. "Sawyer, what's wrong?" She stepped back and looked at him, not a trace of a smile on his face, nothing but thunder and foreboding.

"How much money?"

"What?"

"On the phone right now you said it was a lot of money, I want to know how much money." He sounded angry although she had no idea why.

"Twenty-five thousand dollars," she shrugged, it wasn't a secret.

"Twenty-five thousand dollars," Sawyer repeated, "that's all?" He arched his eyebrow at her. "You really had me fooled, didn't you? Tell me, Becca, was everything a lie? Was it all a game to you? Last night, when you claimed to be oh so innocent, was it all just another lie?"

"Sawyer, I-"

"When your face was flushed and you called my name, Becca," he interrupted, "was it just another lie?" Sawyer's voice rose, and his face flashed with anger. "I would have given you everything," he shook his head slowly as if he wasn't sure who she was anymore, "without question, and you threw it all away for twenty-five thousand dollars. Well, congratulations, I guess you got what you wanted. Get out of my house, and don't you dare come near my kids again or I'll have you arrested." As he turned to leave, Becca snapped out of her horror and made to grab at his arm, realisation dawning on her.

"Sawyer, please, wait," she cried out, but it was in vain, Sawyer had already walked away from her, she could hear him collecting the children, and the ominous click of the front door closing behind him. Just like that, her whole world was gone, and she hadn't even had a chance to explain.

CHAPTER NINE
SAWYER

"Sawyer, we need to talk." His mother stood on his doorstep just as daylight started to streak the dawn.

"Mum now is not a good time," Sawyer ran his hand through his hair, his eyes blurry from a sleepless night. The boys had been impossible to settle last night, waking frequently, calling for Becca, wanting to know where she was and when she was coming back. He couldn't tell them that she would never see them again, instead, he had crooned words of love and comfort and they had finally drifted back to sleep.

"Then make the time," his mother walked past him, casting a glance around the room as she walked through to the kitchen to sit at the table.

"Coffee?" Sawyer offered.

"Please." She waited until he had sat opposite her, both nursing coffee cups before she said anything else. "Sawyer, what did you do to Becca?"

"Mother," there was a warning in Sawyer's tone, "leave it alone."

"No, I will not. I've had her grandmother on the phone to me all night, absolutely distressed, so you tell me, right now

Sawyer, did you or did you not fire Becca?"

"Yes, I fired her." He shrugged, his mother was bound to find out sooner or later.

"Sawyer." How his mother was able to pour so much disappointment and emotion into a single word he would never know. "How could you? That was the absolute last thing that they needed right now, on top of everything else."

"I had my reasons." He didn't elaborate.

"I see." His mother's tone was clipped, he obviously wasn't getting out of this conversation without further explanation.

"I caught her talking to a reporter, selling her story, about the kids, mum, about me, for money. So, yes, I fired her on the spot."

"Sawyer, I don't know what you heard, but believe me, there is no way on earth that Becca would ever go to the press about you or any of us for that matter. Did you ask her about it? Did you even bother to find out why she took this job in the first place? Her mother, a woman none of us has seen in years, managed to rack up twenty-five thousand dollars of debt, in her grandmother's name. Utter slime! I had Gladys in tears on the phone when she first told me, Becca didn't even know the true amount until the other day, Gladys was too embarrassed to tell her that she had been conned by her own daughter. That's why she took this job, to help her grandmother out."

"Twenty-five thousand dollars?" Sawyer felt ill.

"Yes. I offered to pay it off, of course, Gladys is my dearest friend, but you know how proud she is, she refused me outright, told me she didn't need charity. Please tell me that you intend on paying

Becca for the time she worked for you, whatever you might think that she did."

"Mum," Sawyer downed the rest of his coffee and stood, "I've made a terrible mistake. Can you watch Sam and Max please, I need to go out, I won't be long."

"Take all the time you need, just make sure you apologise properly." His mother was no fool, she knew he was off to see Becca. He only hoped that Becca would listen to him and forgive him. It didn't take him long to reach Becca's apartment. On the less affluent side of town, it was a quaint-looking apartment building, a fraction of the size of his. Her grandmother let him in reluctantly, informing him that she would be in her room if they needed her, before walking down the narrow hallway into what he suspected was the only bedroom.

"What do you want?" Becca stared at him, her lips pressed into a firm line, arms crossed over her chest.

"Becca, I'm sorry, I'm so, so sorry. I should never have accused you of talking to a reporter, I should have known you would never do that, I'm sorry, please, can you forgive me?"

"You didn't even give me a chance to explain."

"I know, I'm sorry, I was wrong, I was just so scared, Becca, please. I thought...After what had happened, I thought that we were together and then I walked in and heard you on the phone and I just presumed the worst, I couldn't see straight, I'm sorry."

"I see."

"It wasn't even that you were talking to the reporter, not really, Becca. It was the amount, twenty-five thousand dollars, that's all. That's all I was worth to you? I wanted to give you everything, to share my life with you, and here you were, selling it all for twenty-five thousand dollars, I just felt ill. You see, to me, Becca, you were worth everything."

"Sawyer, don't," Becca warned.

"I've never really been a risk-taker, Becca, I've led a pretty safe life, nowhere near as adventurous as yours. But this is a risk I am willing to take." He stepped closer to Becca, desperate to reach out and take her in his arms, but instead, settled for brushing a stray strand of hair away from her face. "I love you, Becca. I don't know when or how it happened, but you came in and turned my life upside down. I love you. Max and Sam love you. I want my life, my everything, to include you. Please, forgive me for being an idiot?"

"Sawyer, of course, I forgive you." With that Sawyer pulled her into his arms, holding her close, revelling in the feel of her arms wrapped around him, grounding him, reminding him of home. "Please come home with me. Not as my employee," he hastened to add before there could be any confusion, "Becca," Sawyer eased her away from him, dropping to his knee and taking her hand in his. "Marry me, Becca? Share my life, my children, my everything? Stay with me forever, please?"

CHAPTER TEN
BECCA

It was funny how life turned out, Becca thought to herself as she watched Sawyer from across the room. He and his father were currently helping four-year-old Sam to assemble their Christmas train set while five-year-old Max sat at the table with his two grandmas, helping to taste test another batch of Christmas cookies. Becca and Sawyer had been married for two years now, having wed on Christmas Eve the year he had proposed, Sawyer joking that he didn't want to risk being an idiot again and losing her for good. They had sold the penthouse and purchased a sprawling property just out of the city, and closer to his parents. There was a two-bedroom apartment at the back of the property that her grandmother happily moved into, the boys now delighting in having two grandmothers to wrap around their little fingers. Although they had some competition in that area, Becca and Sawyer welcomed their first child together, a daughter, six months ago. As if on cue, Stella cooed in Becca's arms and waved her chubby fist in the air, six pairs of eyes turning to look over at them, love shining brightly.

"Aww, look daddy," Max spoke, "I bet she's sad she can't join us, hey?"

"Give her time, next year she'll be into everything," Sawyer stood and ruffled Max's hair as he passed him. Becca smiled at the action. It had hurt him deeply when the boys had started to call him daddy, he had felt it had betrayed their real father. With Becca's help, he had seen it as an honour, and they often spoke of Sam and Max's real parents with them, the boys secure in the knowledge of Becca and Sawyer's love for them. When Stella had been born, instead of jealousy, the boys had been delighted, convinced that their real parents had sent her down to them. Becca thought it was a lovely idea.

"How's my princess?" He asked once he reached her side, placing a kiss on Stella's head as he took her from Becca.

"Happy as can be," Becca snuggled closer to her husband, "as am I." She leant up and kissed him on the cheek. "I love you, Sawyer, Merry Christmas."

"I love you too, Becca, Merry Christmas."

THE END

About The Author

An international bestselling and award-winning author of sweet contemporary romance, Kathleen's novels showcase thought-provoking plots and strong emotions that have been likened to a Hallmark movie. Featuring feisty heroines and strong heroes, where everyone gets a happily ever after. To discover more about Kathleen: https://linktr.ee/KathleenRyder

Join Kathleen Online

Instagram

BookBub

Read More of Kathleen's Books

www.ingramcontent.com/pod-product-compliance
Lightning Source LLC
Chambersburg PA
CBHW070330120726
47909CB00008B/2666